How to Bury a Boy at Sea

Phil Goldstein

STILL
HOUSE
PRESS

Copyright © 2022 by Phil Goldstein.
FIRST EDITION
All rights reserved.

No part of this book may be reproduced without written permission from the publisher.

All inquiries may be directed to:
   Stillhouse Press
   4400 University Drive, 3E4
   Fairfax, VA 22030
   www.stillhousepress.org

Stillhouse Press is an independent, student- and alumni-run nonprofit press based out of Northern Virginia and established in collaboration with the Fall for the Book festival.

Cover image: Jeffrey Rivers

The epigraph to this book is from "The Red Poppy" from *The Wild Iris* by Louise Glück. Copyright © 1992 by Louise Glück. Used by permission of HarperCollins Publishers.

Library of Congress Control Number: 2021950603
ISBN-13: 978-1-945233-14-2

I

We Never Went to the Beach When I Was a Boy	1
There's No Place Like	2
Changing	3
My Father's Lessons	4
How My Mother Made the Soup on Rosh Hashanah	5
Luggage	6
Silence	7
Immature Answers	8
A Prayer for Repentance	9
Conversations with My Mother	10
The Other Brother Speaks	11
Pack for a Trip of Indeterminate Length	12
Fragile	13
In the North Country, the Wind Howls Hard	14
Growth	15
What a Bed Takes In	16

II

Night Cruises	19
What the House Sees	20
Wandering in Search of Truth	21
Bright, Bright Boy	22
Starlight	23
The Theater Provides Its Review	25
Form & Void	26
This Is My Story	27
My Lover Appears as an Avenging Angel After I Tell Her I Was Abused	29
The Last Act	30

III

The Island	33
The Lover as Unexpected Glaciologist	34
On Masculinity	35
I Rise from the Hills	36
The Parents Tend to Their Beautiful Garden	37
An Apology & My Response	38
Repayment in Kind	39
Confessions of a Synagogue	40
A Ritual for Mourning	41
I Wait for the Wind's Return	42
What My Mother Misses, As Told to Her Sister	43

IV

A Dream of the Pirate Captain's Demise	47
The Exorcism of a Boy	48
Is This What Sex Is?	49
The Edge of the Summit	50
My Father Is So Disappointed	51
A Note to My Younger Self	52
Gibraltar	53
What Wakes a Mother in the Middle of the Night	54
The Grief Eater	55

V

Sunken No More	59
The Sound of Blood Flowing Through Me	60
The Unburying	61
Memories of My Childhood (If They Had Been Photographed)	62
Love During a Storm, Delighted	63
Rhapsody in Periwinkle	64
Late Night Call with God	65
Our Wedding	66
I Find Happiness	67
We Are the Flowers in That Good Earth	68
The Aftertaste of the Wind	69
How to Bury a Boy at Sea	70
Acknowledgements	73
Resources for Survivors	75

For Jenny, my rock.

And for the survivors of child sexual abuse, wherever you are.

CONTENT WARNING:
This text deals heavily with child sexual abuse.

"I speak because I am shattered."

—Louise Glück, "The Red Poppy"

I

We Never Went to the Beach When I Was a Boy

He & I are traveling to an alien shore, alone.
He commands me to get into our tiny boat.
My feet stay stuck, stakes buried in the sand.

The waves roll in, briny & filled with seaweed,
water that makes me gag when I get
washed underneath.

He pushes me aboard,
then clambers in himself—
eager, a bird learning to fly.

Gulls cry in the gray blanket overhead.
He has the oars.
We are rowing now.

There's No Place Like

I am brought back to that diamond,
less of a park & more a spit of green in suburbia.

We all gathered to play, not really to see
who would win. We simply wanted

to be free. That's what children long for.
Don't they? I've heard that in the years since.

In a small clearing there stood a solid rock wall
curved like an outfield fence. This was our arena.

We didn't have enough boys to
cover every position, but we made it work.

On we played, inning after inning,
kicking instead of swinging. That was safer.

As time stretched out in a summer haze
the peculiar order of our configuration

placed the path to victory on
my slender legs & awkward feet.

My older brother, the winning run,
was standing on a pile of rocks that passed
for third, calling out encouragement.
He had my back, in this neighborhood, in this idyll.

He said he knew I could do it, had it in me.
He bucked me up, calling out:
Send me home,
send me home...

Home.
It was always
with you, my big brother.

Changing

Surrounded by the kind of metallic turquoise blue
only found on school gym lockers, I clutch
the towel tight around my 12-year-old waist.
I drop my jeans rimmed with my underwear,
push them aside like armor. Now comes the moment
of the most intense vulnerability. I reach
for my bathing suit with my left hand, my right
still grasping the cinch around my waist. I slip one foot
inside the left trunk, then the right, crouch & pull
up, up, up my legs.

My Father's Lessons

My father taught me how to throw & catch a ball, but my lack of coordination always caught up with me. He taught me to say *please* & *thank you*, to respect & obey my elders: they know what's best. He worked late & hard for the four of us. He taught me the value of honest labor. He taught me how to tear bread to feed the ducks down at Foxwood Pond. He taught me how to play chess, the favored game of his father, my namesake.

Most vividly, I recall lessons on how to ride a bike. We went to the empty asphalt oval outside the school. He taught me how to balance, how to keep moving, how to stay upright amid fear that washed over me—fear of falling, breaking so many bones. Eventually, as it usually happens when a child is learning to ride a bike, I fell & tumbled going around a curve, my forearm scraped & bloodied.

My father taught me how to get up, dimpled with dust & gravel.

How My Mother Made the Soup on Rosh Hashanah

I am standing next to you,
almost attached at the hip,
following your movements, Mama.

You are preparing all of the ingredients
for matzoh ball soup, using a recipe that stretches back
to some long-dead shtetl in Poland.

I cannot grasp the history. All I can think of is the smell
of the broth, carrots, celery & dough as you bounce
around the cramped kitchen, a ball of your own neurotic energy.

It is time to say Shana Tova to cousins, aunts & uncles.
I have finished making everything presentable.
I am holding back & watching you whisk magic into being.

Your pot is a cauldron of history & comfort; golden & shimmering.
A pinch of sugar here, a few grinds of pepper there, & now
we let it simmer. We let it simmer. We let it simmer.

We wait for something to change.

Luggage

I am a hand-me-down, with an ancient bronze zipper
that snags a bit as it glides across the top.
I carry deep in my belly dimpled cardigans, tchotchkes, memories.

I have so many memories I want to forget but never will.
Right there, on the cracked gray floor, the violation.
The shag carpet saw it, the washing machine as well.
We whisper about it when the lights click off.

If I carry something with me wherever I go does it become
part of me?

Will I slowly lose definition, become
a person, a man with a mouth,
someone who has the ability to speak but chooses not to?

Silence

No one at school or synagogue or anywhere asked me:

Are you alright?

Is there anything going on at home you want to talk about?

Immature Answers

My brother told our parents
I did not punch or kick or run.
Is that what he'd imagine I'd do, at 10?

I never said no.
He said I said
yes with my eyes
as they darted & fluttered like hummingbirds,
yes with silent lips
as they opened & received all that was pushed into them,
yes with my hands
as they were maneuvered over dark & thick-matted hills,
yes with my tongue
as it swirled around inviting like a song,
yes with my silence
as it wordlessly welcomed in more,
always more.

A Prayer for Repentance

How can someone atone for a sin they cannot name?

It was Yom Kippur. The four of us donned formal wear.
Mom was anxious & had to double-check the locks, making us late.
Dad yelled, cursing the heavens. Our annual ritual—
fasting, & then rushing out to Wendy's at 4 o'clock to break.

How can someone atone for a sin they cannot name?

Among the crowded, ticketed, gussied-up masses,
we filed in to pray, to atone
for our sins. I was 11, obediently taking in
the words of teshuvah:

For transgressions against God, the Day of Atonement atones;
but for transgressions of
one human being against another,
the Day of Atonement does not atone
until they have made peace with one another.

How can someone atone for a sin they cannot name?
How can I forgive my brother for a sin he will never confess—
not to me or our parents?

After the afternoon service, we got our single combos:
square burgers, golden & salty fries, ice-cold Sprite.
I squirted the ketchup into two rimmed paper cups.
We devoured in near silence.

Conversations with My Mother

A Monday. We peel
off into the highway to discuss
Europa which, we now know,
has a liquid ocean swirling under a thick crust of ice.

A Thursday. We speed
along & Pakistan's nuclear tests are the topic.
You tell me of how scary it was to grow up
in the shadow of nuclear holocaust—
the utter pointlessness of duck-&-cover drills.

A Friday. A week before
my eleventh birthday, we chat about
the International Criminal Court.
How do you punish crimes so horrible
a normal process simply will not do?

A Wednesday. The night before,
Roger Maris's record had fallen in St. Louis.
I had watched it on a 10-inch Sony
when I should have been asleep.
You told me about the glory days of the Yankees growing up.

On our journeys my back would melt into the seat.
Hyper-articulate, I conversed with you about
Desert Fox, Matthew Shepherd, the Good Friday Accords.
I never spilled a word about
my truest, hidden self.

The encyclopedic, voracious reader—that was your second son.
I could not tell you what your first son
had done to me, was doing, would do.
Let's talk about the arrest of Pinochet.

The Other Brother Speaks

Even before they shipped me off to Special Ed in a special school, I had enough sense to know that
my brother & I were very different. He spoke like an adult in full sentences at such a tender age,
it filled me with madness & wonder. How could it all be so easy for him? I knew he'd always glow

in their eyes, like the idol Indiana Jones tries to steal in the Peruvian jungle, golden & radiant,
a sun to warm their pale Tri-State skin in January. At night, I would peer out from the top bunk
at home across the small parking lot to the enclosed dumpsters, remembering the
broken beer bottles we passed by amid games of Manhunt, their necks sheared off

in crooked peaks like a brown city skyline, the faint aroma of lager clinging to the jagged edges amid
a deeper bouquet of rancid chicken & sour milk. I had not consciously resolved that
I would touch him, transform him, steal the idol, unleash a rumbling

in the deep. I wanted & I wanted & I wanted & I just wanted to *do*, but I hadn't thought of what
that something would be or what it would even mean. But breaking my brother is what I wound up
doing anyway. Maybe, I figured, if I could make him as broken as me, they would see us in the same
damp light that seemed to cling to my skin like film. After I broke him

if they ever wanted to drink from my brother again they'd just have to get used to the taste
of blood on their lips.

Pack for a Trip of Indeterminate Length

I wondered as we started out on the voyage
if we'd be wearing pants this time,
the kind—white & linen—that Santiago does in *The Old Man and the Sea*,
a book whose cover called out to me
from the wooden shelf in the public library downtown.

I'm not sure how long we will be here, in this.
I should have packed shorts for the afternoon sun,
or a sweater to keep me warm
when the wind chewed through me at night.
The days flow onward, an endless line of swells.

Will it be winter soon, or someday?
Will what little I have with me last?
What if it doesn't? All I have left is
him & the waves
rising & falling all around me, on & on & on.

Fragile

to my parents

I get the feeling, still, that you two think
he is a fragile egg & I am a rock:
unbreakable, unshakable, golden.
That's what our name means, from the German: *gold stone*.

Let me tell you,
I was not as resilient as you thought.
I was not an adult trapped in a child's body.
I was a child trapped in a child's body, unable to move.

Why can't you see I crack & cry & break & bleed?
I am the egg. He is the fox,
scratching at the tiny doorway,
looking for more, hungry.

In the North Country, the Wind Howls Hard

We hurtled around the curve of Lake Ontario,
so deep & wide it seemed like the ocean.

It looked like the ocean, moved like the ocean.
But salt water wasn't churning in its heart. It was fresh, pure.

I was obsessed with collecting Pokémon cards, the Jungle set.
That seemed like a good distraction.

It was the summer of 1999, & I was hunting
for Snorlax, Flareon & Clefable.

Trading cards can be so important for a 12-year-old.
A world to escape into, where the monsters lie flat on a table.

We had come from Niagara Falls, the four of us.
All that pressure pouring down, water on rock on water.

In a bland hotel in Toronto I shared a bed with my brother.
We did what brothers normally do on trips.

I fell asleep with my heart dancing around my ribs,
remembering when we laid together in secret.

At home it was heightened, flowing, surreal, a jumble.
North of the border, I was stick-straight.

We walked along the lake, two pairs, & the wind
blew through me, but I was strong & unruffled. I was strong.

Growth

I could tell the way he touched me was
strange.

He told me, & told me, that it was normal.
How could something that felt so good be wrong?

We did the normal routines—washing our hands,
clearing our plates, rising for the Shema—out in the open.

We face in the direction of the ancient walls, turning toward the light of Adonai.
We are a holy congregation, twisting ourselves to be in the brightness.

We stand as one, no separation between our bodies & our lips, unified
in the voice that we call out with in that soaring sanctuary.

In the open fields, everyone can see how you grow,
how you take in sunlight & breathe.

The two of us became intertwined when nobody could see.
Our roots & limbs grew in the darkness.

I didn't know then that foxgloves & violets bloom in shade.
What is it like to be a foxglove, to be a violet?

What a Bed Takes In

The things I've seen would make me tear out my eyes, if I had any.
What I've felt, from so many years ago, still stains me
deep in every fiber of my being
no matter how many times I am washed.

I saw a boy, thin of frame, drawn into my center
by a larger one, stronger, who pushed
the little one's head under my folds, & there it
stayed for quite some time, bobbing like a cork in the Atlantic.

All of these years later, I want to swallow myself whole
for letting it just happen, right on top of me,
for not shouting, for not even breathing a word.
How does one recover from witnessing such pain?

Will I ever tell you, dear reader, of all that I know?
Can you wring it out of me, like water or semen?
Will I collapse in a heap, damp at your feet?
Can you stretch me in the rack, tortured & taut?

Even then, what am I?
Certainly not what you see & touch every day. Surely,
nothing so neat & serene & soft
could hold so much inside.

II

Night Cruises

My world is only slightly wider than a twin bed
framed by endless ocean.
So much seems unnatural, but I know one thing:
long nights are coming.

The stars above are the only fixed points
to hold. I grasp for anything else that's secure, but—no.
I don't control the oars, or even
where I sit, when I cross my legs.

When I wake, sore & lightened, he is still
rowing & smiling.

What the House Sees

I watched him as he approached my front door. Awkward,
still too short for his age.
The trees were on fire. It was October. They glowed
crimson, tangerine, & amber, their decaying embers
hurtling themselves to the ground, silent & dreamlike.
I feared for my safety & I feared for his.
I was just getting to know him. He seemed
fragile, an icicle dangling from my shingles, slender & dripping.
I did not know what he wished, or where
he had been, but he seemed distant, lost
in his own worlds. I suppose that's normal for boys his age.
To imagine you are someone else, untouched

by the familiar. I wondered if he wished he was
like the oaks & maples—setting himself alight.
Everyone witnessing
the flames his body made, set against the sky.

Wandering in Search of Truth

Where were Your plagues when I needed them,
to take the first-born son so he could no longer hurt me?
I stand before You,

Your word, Your Truth, Your people,
as a boy about to become a man,
who stopped being a boy years before.

I have so many questions for You.

Where was Your parting of the sea
while I was being torn apart?
Who are You to me—then, now, & always?

I do not know. Like so many others
I was condemned to wander the desert.
All I know is the taste of sand.

Bright, Bright Boy

I was desperate for light.
I filled my veins at night with a luminous substance.
I imagined myself on a stage, at a podium, on a pedestal—
anywhere I could shine & reflect my light back home.
I had not yet read in a schoolbook about nuclear shadows,
when the blast's intense heat burns everything around a disintegrated person,
bleaching the stone, leaving their imprint.
No amount of sunshine can ever erase such a silhouette.

Starlight

I

I walk through the forest, alone at dusk, the pine needles making a blanket underfoot, the tree roots radiate out as mountain ranges, protecting small valleys of moss & leaves. The light fades between the trees, orange shafts growing dimmer. The only sound is a rustle of the branches in the wind & the crunch of autumn in my wake.

I don't have a compass, just a vague notion that I should follow the North Star, for stars won't do me any good without a destination, a home.

II

Under the covers, back in time, I was a space pilot in a saga of my own creation, fighting off a ceaseless invasion, my arms outstretched like laser cannons, blasting the monsters trying to dominate my home territory.

III

I was left to make my way alone. Everyone was so sure of my sure-footedness, my ability to shine no matter how deep the night fell. What stands out in the sky above your home is what you can see. I didn't know then that 85 percent of the universe is dark matter.

IV

I would race to the library to take out every book I could find on astronomy, the planets, moons & stars, projecting myself into space at the speed of light down the hallway to get lost in another world outside my own. Under cover, under the covers, I could be hidden & be anything, take on a new face, a different life, float above it all, a stranger to gravity & everything else pulling me down.

V

I will never go back to that school. I live in the forest now. It breathes shadow, alive with nocturnal activity, noises only heard at night that pierce my mind & slice my comfort. The trees take on wild aspects, strange tall creatures towering over me, casting odd shapes from gnarled branches—what is this place? It is where defenseless creatures fall prey to venom & suffer, wounded, caressed by the night.

Above, the stars cast their light down, pinpricks of brightness that have been traveling for so long through space & time they are ancient by now, yet here they are guiding my way out, not home but to safety by way of the sky.

The light that was always there always will be. Come, old friends, dance with me among the trees.

The Theater Provides Its Review

Who else could unbutton a shirt onstage & not recall
buttons coming undone, one by one, in his brother's bed?
Who else could charm the audience with his verve
yet curdle with dread when the bedroom door closed?

For years he kept up such a magnificent façade, the inner world faded
into nothingness, merged with the outward gaze.
He could never let his audience down, let the mask drop even for a moment.
Where did he sink, in that deeper shadow, that liquid dark?

I honestly don't know. I just recall the actor
who never betrayed
his own inner turmoil. It was always the character
who shone.

Form & Void

I am staring at a computer screen.
The past is staring back at me.

It is at once just a clickable PDF form
& my deepest shame, dripping in the dark.

I am thirty, surrounded by coworkers in an office.
I am ten years old, & I am alone.

The form interrogates me, asks me plainly in black & white:
Abuse history. Two words freighted with steel & lead.

Physical, emotional, neglect, sexual abuse. The options. *P, E, N, S.*
I am seized by the tight grip of memory.

I am back in the basement, on the cool gray stone floor.
I am holding my brother's erect penis in my hand. I am twelve.

The form stares back at me, expressionless.
Its professionalism is detached, but comforting. It does not judge.

I do not want to lie. I've lied enough. I fear &
worry what will happen if I keep lying.

What if I lie & then my therapist, my first, finds out?
The fear of discovery purchased my silence. Now it pays for my voice.

What if I lie & this never gets solved & I can't have sex?
What if this never gets solved & I end up alone, again?

Age? I fill in *10-12*. Type? I mark an S. By whom?
My older brother. Duration of Abuse? *Two & a half years.*

Reported? Y/N. *No.*
Outcome of report. *Left blank.*

This Is My Story

For such a forbidding place it had nice upholstery.
Soft lighting. White noise. Welcoming voice.
A breeze. Tissues. So many boxes of tissues.

When I sat down, the first question I got was:
What brought you here?

Well, I've been having issues in my relationship with my girlfriend.
True enough. A curious shift in her chair.
My eyes darted quickly to the painting of a calm ocean.

What kind of issues?

It got caught in my throat at first, a piece of chicken wing
gobbled down too quickly. I stammered:
Sex issues. You know, we, um, we,
we've been having issues with having sex.

Then it rose up in me, acid memory
of what the truth was, the truth I had already confessed
on that damn form staring back at me.

Starting when I was 10
my older brother, he…

The breath caught in my chest, a mountain on my ribs,
the walls pushed in, crushing the desk & couches.
Think of that calm ocean, I told myself, think of the azure water.

He sexually abused me, I gulped out to her. But that's not why I'm here.
I'm here because I want to improve my relationship. I just
don't want to lose my girlfriend.

I'm so sorry that happened to you. Thank you
for trusting me with that information.
The whole room exhaled, stopped contracting.
I felt an unknown, unknowable golden substance fill my lungs.
Felt it rush to my fingertips, unclench them from my thighs.

I know why I'm here.
I'm here so I can be a man. With my girlfriend.
I'm not a boy. I'm not a boy.
I am a man. I'm a man, goddamn it.

My Lover Appears as an Avenging Angel After I Tell Her I Was Abused

A piece of the sun brought down to the earth, she is capable of leveling mountains & flash-
boiling oceans. With a single question, she becomes an owl in Maine, knocking snow off a pine

to reveal the bare black branch & grip it. Now she knows why I cry so easily, why
the bed is cold, why I shrink from a man into a boy at the slightest slight. She is bright:
the sun creeping over the mountain's edge. My eyes start to burn & everything grows quiet.
She has the power to pulverize, the might to rip hearts from chests, eyes that see

in the dark. She spreads the anger of her wings, but her hand rests gently on my arm.
She will not shrink from this fight.

The Last Act

On a cold April New Jersey Saturday, I was consumed
by a bad case of backstage jitters
at the wedding of the brother
who I once slept under in a bunkbed.

I knew it was time
to use all those years of practice
for this one final play, this role of a lifetime
to toast my brother, hug him as if he were
my brother.
The audience sat rapt, & waited.

I had practiced my lines for weeks,
a pantomime of affection.
I knew which marks to hit, when to pause for laughter.

Champagne glimmered in two hundred glasses
under the ballroom's bright klieg lights.
I began my performance,
slipped
back to the rhythms
that governed my life for twenty years.

I dipped our childhood in amber, elided
the truth & anything dark,
focusing on summers spent playing kickball in makeshift diamonds.
Then came the crucial turn.

I extolled my brother's virtues, with such seeming sincerity:
his work ethic, empathy, generosity, humility, & love.
I choked back black tar. That was the last time I stood onstage
in service of someone else's story.

III

The Island

One day we spotted an island.
A sandy cloud
shimmering in the sunlight like glass.

There was a group of boys
playing with each other on the beach,
in the way boys play, losing track of time & laughing

until doubled over on their knees.
I wished I could shatter our boat by crying out
& then swim to shore to be with them, to be one of them,

to be just a boy once again. That would be a dream.
That would be an endless summer day.
But the boys & the sand receded from view

as the sun dipped beneath the horizon.
It was then that I remembered
we were our own island & always would be.

The Lover as Unexpected Glaciologist

Our bed is a river of ice, cleaving
more & more every day.
I am in a cave deep inside, without
even a penguin to keep me company.

When will he return?
When will I get to cast my stories on the walls?
All I want sometimes, is for him
to breathe into my neck & tickle me deep.

Instead, his tremulous hands fill me
with an undying dread.
No matter how many eons pass or where we flow, he never asks
how I got here, what my geology can reveal.

On Masculinity

You're not a real man if you write poetry—
real men aren't named Wilde & Whitman & Ginsberg
& Baldwin & Auden & O'Hara.

You're not a real man if you act in plays,
dancing & singing, a total fairy
onstage, under the lights, staring into darkness.

You're not a real man if you wait
until you're twenty-one to be inside a woman &
don't know what you're doing at first.

You're not a real man if you lose your erection
again & again & again,
with different women in different beds.

You're not a real man if you admit
to being abused. Real men don't let others
make them do anything.

You're not a real man if you tell
your parents of your deepest shame, the truth you hid, letting you
compartmentalize, bury & then excel.

You're not a real man unless you tell your son
that he's not ten years old anymore.
Accountability is something he'll need to get himself.

You're not a real man unless you steal a boy's innocence,
pocket his soul for a prize, evince no real remorse
& blow aside his pain like cigarette smoke.

I Rise from the Hills

I never said, "I do, I do, I do."
I said to myself, Don't tell mom. Don't tell. Don't.
I never knew anything but to be afraid.

Once again, the windswept hills remind me
there is no direction home.
Just amber light, still waters, the hush of smoke
in the tolerance of my own guilt. I do mourn the loss of my will.

Reluctant, neglected, plunged into denial,
tattered edge meeting edge.

Now, I know I can ascend full of grace.
People seem to be less afraid.
Lots of people are starting to ask questions.
It's becoming hard to avoid the questions.

The Parents Tend to Their Beautiful Garden

We are the gardeners, the overseers, you see.
We have two flowers in our garden: an orchid & a dandelion.
We knew from early on that the orchid needed to be misted,
kept safe & tended with the utmost care,
or else it would wilt under the natural light of the sky.

Our dandelion can sprout up anywhere,
a cartoon sun unfolding itself atop a pale green leaning ladder.
Did you know that it can thrive amid thunderstorms &
the battering of summer hail,
growing even without supervision?

We sometimes asked ourselves in the recesses of the night,
What precise lattice work of genes & stress
gave bloom to our delicate, frustrating orchid?
What epigenome & DNA & thunder danced
& wove its soft, pale frame into being?

The dandelion came after, small but hearty at first, then
glowing in the heavy summer air
in the fields, on the hills & the small strip of grass between
safety & all lies underneath the ground in wait.
We worried for the orchid, & carried it lightly

from one specialist botanist to the next for attention
to its lateral sepal, labellum & petals,
this precious, fragile jewel of a flower.
We did not notice the orchid's roots strangling the dandelion
beneath the soil. We do not live underground.

After all, the dandelion did not wither & die.
In fact, it thrived, as dandelions are wont to do.
Would we have cut out the orchid had we known?
Who can say? It's a hypothetical exercise
we'd prefer not to think about.

We are wonderful gardeners—loving, nurturing caretakers.
Shoo. Shoo. Leave our garden be.

An Apology & My Response

Dear

First and foremost I want to start off by letting you know that IM SORRY **(Are you, really? I want to see your remorse drip from your brow)** for all the things I put you through when we were younger, both physically and mentally **(You can't even name them. Say: you molested me)**. I know these were wrong things to do **(Then why did you do them?)** and I'm truly sorry for any pain and hurt that I caused you **(You'll never know how much)**. I know that our relationship hasn't really been a good one **(What relationship? What foundation was there?)** and the last thing I want is for us not to have any communication **(I wish I could separate down to the molecules in my DNA everything that binds me to you so that you were actually a stranger I never knew)**. Growing up for me wasn't easy, I had a lot of problems and got into trouble a lot **(So that excuses you making me suck your dick?)**. The last thing I wanted to do was hurt you **(What, then, did you mean to do?)**, but I was a mixed up kid and didn't understand how very wrong it was **(At 17, you didn't know it was wrong?)**. I have been in therapy about this myself to help me deal with my anxieties and part of therapy has made me realize that what I did to you was wrong **(You realized this at the age of 35?)**. Again, I'm truly sorry for any pain and hurt that I caused you. I hope you can take this sincere apology from my heart to yours and hope that we can move on from the past and work on the future.

Sincerely,

Repayment in Kind

I want to draw my blade from its sheath
& slice you at a harsh angle across your face—
mark my territory
& brand you with cold steel—
so that you will never again be able to
hide who you are,
the depths where you pulled me down,
everything you stole when I was
too young to know what I had to lose.

My wounds were invisible but grievous,
unknown even to me,
the equivalent of spiritual internal bleeding,
dripping inside for twenty years,
a well of deep memory & hushed water.

In our parents' bed & on the unfinished basement floor
you are a mountain & I am
skin & bones, my ribs visible on
milky skin, crushed like
meal to feed your desires.

I stare down below at
what you're doing to me, not knowing why, really,
only because you want to.
Why are you doing this? I will never know.
Does it feel good to be so in control of me
when your grip is loose on so much else?

I never asked for your touch,
the same way a fly never asks to be destroyed.
It happened because
some force larger than me willed it so.
I, too, am a force now,
like vengeance, doom, fate.
You won't know when my sword will swing,
but I promise you, it will be
the sharpest thing you've ever felt.

Confessions of a Synagogue

He entered me as a boy
countless times, in Sabbath morning light,
in Friday nights' holy wonder. I wonder
what he was thinking in those hardest of years
as he sat down inside my sanctuary to sing
L'chah Dodi, to welcome the Bride.
Sing the words:
Safeguard & remember in a single utterance.

I safeguard & I remember him, this bright
boy, 11 years old, & how he would race
at the end of Kabbalat Shabbat to the Oneg
for rainbow cookies & grape juice. What bitter tastes
must have been lingering idly in his mouth.
Maybe he thought he could drown them with sweets.
Have another piece of succulent challah.
Tear it up & cast each piece away for your sins for Tashlich.

In my halls & classrooms he learned of the Torah,
of the words of the People of the Book. He learned of Abraham
& how Adonai tested his faith by commanding him to
sacrifice his son. What do those words truly mean?
Sacrifice. Son. What did he give up
to his older brother, besides his innocence?
How many times did the family of four sit in a row with so much
space in between them, together & yet wholly apart?

Sing, sing, welcome the Sabbath Bride:
"Arise! Leave from the midst of the turmoil;
Long enough have you sat in the valley of tears.
He will take great pity upon you compassionately.
Shake yourself free, rise from the dust ...
Rouse yourself, rouse yourself.
Your light is coming. Rise up & shine."

I was his sanctuary, but I could not keep him safe.

A Ritual for Mourning

The rabbis say we Jews place the stones on the grave
for many reasons, some lost to time,
others shrouded in superstition: to keep the soul
down where it belongs; to honor the dead
by marking our presence; to spark a bit of the departed
to visit with us during our mourning; or, perhaps, my favorite,
because stones last, they are repositories of memory,
cracked bits of mountain that hold eons in their veins.
They carry the light of life, the joy of the past.
But their cool underbellies suck up the dirt & rot of the earth, too.
The stones are a testament to all that came before,
Permanent, hard, & painful, like shrapnel waiting to explode.
Why do we block phone calls, drift with the current,
make new homes & place stones?
The rabbis would offer many answers, but
once a thing is done it becomes
one more stone to be placed upon another.

I Wait for the Wind's Return

On my better days, I wonder
when I will learn to stop bracing
my body against something strong & powerful
in the air that never comes.

What My Mother Misses, As Told to Her Sister

I miss him, I miss him every day.
He never replies to my messages.
I'm sorry, I really am.

I don't know how he can still be so upset with me.
How was I supposed to react?
Look, I'm not a goddamn mind reader!
He never gave us any sign. He was just on autopilot.

How could you suggest that? I didn't know.
I couldn't act on something I didn't *know about*.
I don't know why he didn't tell us.
Why would he be afraid? Why would he be silent about, you know, the abuse?
He was so smart, so articulate. He was *always talking*.

Look, we knew what a dysfunctional, difficult child looked like.
He was never anything close to that.
He never showed any signs that anything was wrong—just the opposite.
How were we supposed to know that he felt like he needed to be perfect?

We never told him he needed to be perfect.
We're not mind readers.
We wouldn't have gotten mad at him.
We would have moved heaven & earth to stop it.
We would have done something.
I don't know—we would have done something.

He told me we shouldn't have assumed he was so emotionally mature.
I guess that was a mistake on our part.
He should have told us. He should have told us.
That was his mistake.

IV

A Dream of the Pirate Captain's Demise

I wish I had the strength
of twenty men, the kind who could plot & carry out
a mutiny, a rebellion against a tyrannical captain
who works his crew until
they're nothing but a collection of shadows & open sores.

This collective force would bind
him & coerce him into drinking a dram of truth serum
so that he couldn't hide behind his silver tongue & rotting teeth.
We'd make his eyes burn with sorrow & then with fear
as we cut off a sliver of his forearm
to serve as chum for the sharks off our starboard.

How we'd watch him plead, wriggle, bawl,
stripped of all his power, authority & finery,
his creased hat & gold earrings.
Even his clothes tossed aside.
What a sight for the boys.

My reverie is broken & I
get seasick for the second time this week.

The Exorcism of a Boy

I am the only Jewish exorcist there is, except
I don't know the ritual.
All I know is I want to cast this demon out,
a flock of sparrows fleeing in November.

Can you who are witness
to this eerie ceremony help me?
If I say the words in precise order
will the black ink dissolve from my pupils like watercolor?

I create my own liturgy,
my odes to the power of nature, my pleas to grace:

Burn this rot out of me, the way sun melts fog
as the morning unspools itself.

Give me the strength to crush mountains
& grind the rubble to dust.

Let my voice resound like a hurricane of birdsong
to drown out the chorus of sinners.

Break the hands of all those who shackle me
so that they cannot grasp anything soft or tender.

Is This What Sex Is?

My hand was on his penis, his hand was on my penis.
My mouth was on his penis, his mouth was on my penis.
I stared up at the ceiling
& I wondered.

Now, when I am with you, I wish
I wasn't betrayed
by my body as it seeks to connect with yours.
Will I always be
trapped in my parents' bed,
staring up at the ceiling?
I wonder.

I lie next to you, my love, & you lie next to me,
the silence thick & suffocating.
When I try, I am often deflated
to the size of a boy, fearing touch
& I wonder.

You sit up & ask
Is this what sex is going to be?

The Edge of the Summit

I cried a mountain of salt & climbed to its summit.
With a slight nudge & a subtle shifting of the terrain, it could break
every bone in my body.

That's real power—the unspoken threat of force,
the promise of a tortured, drawn-out demise
for having the temerity to tell the truth.

My Father Is So Disappointed

I spent so many years building this boy into a man, I am not
going to let him be torn down like some poster on a bedroom wall.

I am trying, I have always tried, to do what is right, to teach both of my sons what is right.
Clearly, with one, I failed. How could he leave our family name

bloodied & splintered in the snow, a shattered deer carcass displayed to everyone?
What was he thinking

when he did this? Certainly not what I taught him about being an honorable man, a mensch.
He did this behind my back,

this betrayal. This horrible, cowardly, selfish act. How could he expose
something so private, so publicly? On Facebook! I just don't know.

My older son? Well, he had some troubles, but he's different now.
I welcome him with open arms.

A Note to My Younger Self

You can't be saved, not now. You must hang on
until the day you are strong enough to climb out.

You can't be blamed
for staying beneath the water.
There, quiet felt like peace.

You must navigate a thread
so small it's practically invisible,
the line between what you feel & what you can say:
pushing up a jagged wall everywhere you tread.

You are just a boy, you are just a boy, you are just a boy,
you can't be anything but a boy.

Gibraltar

I see you now in the hazy veil of painted twilight,
a shadow but not a terror.

You were the monster of my childhood
whose hand-me-downs once kept me warm.

Sometimes, the flash & force of memory shoots me
straight back, deeper than I want to go.

The way I lie down in a bed is enough to take me
to the times when you led me to lie with you.

I ache the way a tree must ache when it is chopped &
left to stand, gashed open, in a summer thunderstorm.

I stand now in a field with the sun bleeding away to violet.
I stand knowing what I have endured, what I can endure.

I am a promontory, gauzy in sunshine, the sea lapping green below.
You are a shadow passing over my face—a cloud, a memory.

What Wakes a Mother in the Middle of the Night

I have been forced to choose
between my jaw & my tongue, my eyes & my nose.
Which wound will I create in my body?
Which hole will I make permanent & glaring?

Has the sky ever been so much like me?
Out here in the desert, devoid of light pollution,
the Milky Way is a smoky fissure, curling overhead,
a wound in the sky, bleeding light.

What can a mother do to stop her sons
from hurting one another? What can a mother do to unmake
a tear in the side of a continent?
How do you repair that kind of gash?

Amid the cacti & armadillos, the earth shudders
every time I move. It vomits dirt, the kind shoveled
on a casket after the prayers have been intoned.
The sky will never stop bleeding down.

The Grief Eater

He has many names, but what He does never varies.
He feeds off the untimely deaths of children, among other delicacies.

He feasts on families torn asunder with the hunger of a ravenous wolf.
He eagerly devours silent agonies. I have the bite marks to prove it.

Spectral face unseen, hooded & cloaked.
He has stalked us for millennia, & me for decades.

He towers over even the tallest of men—*good god!* you might say—
yet He is anything but. He has but one malignant purpose.

He swoops in, a shadowy rocket, having targeted His prey.
Pain is His sustenance & what He multiplies in His wake.

I remember the first time I saw His eel of a tongue
as He salivated over the cold sweat on my hairless chest.

He could sense it inside of me: a glass door shattered but still intact.
He would treat every shard of me as a morsel. *Mmmmm.*

I did not give Him the satisfaction of crumbling. I ran.
I changed my face & buried any trace of my scent.

I was cunning quarry. I was a haunted, hunted boy who
became a haunted, hunted man. Eventually, He found me.

I stood & ran no more. He fluttered. I told Him, *You've lost.*
I bled it out on my own. There is nothing more for you to drink.

V

Sunken No More

When I would get seasick, I would dive
down below to vomit in the ocean & wash it off all at once.
Then I would sink beneath our rowboat until I had lost the light.

Buried at the bottom of the sea, encased
in layers of damage & debris—centuries'—I sat with the pressure
of incalculable fathoms upon me, crushed into the ocean floor.

For ages, no one dared
probe my depths,
not even me, a denizen of the deep.

Hardened, seafaring explorers knew this area to be
nothing more than a blank spot on their atlases.
Then, bubbling up from the dark,

first a trickle then an underwater flood,
the pressure releases & the pieces
begin to break free.

I am rising, driving, kicking, pushing
toward the surface.
I break & breach,

glimmering in the warm sunlight,
barnacles & edges pouring water as I splash down
again on the surface, floating but not adrift.

The Sound of Blood Flowing Through Me

for Jenny

The trees drip leaves from their mouths,
goldenrod, oxblood, apricot, ruby. They fall
like snow as we crunch our way higher.

The wind rushes through the trail, a breath
of October that finds its way
into the small spaces between our intertwined fingers.

We are climbing, trudging, stopping, walking together.
There is no one else who knows the rhythm
of the way I hike like you do, no one who knows

I stumble like a klutz on rocks sometimes.
I march ahead at other intervals, jumping over tree roots
buried in a pile of honey-colored foliage.

You chide me, we laugh, we plow on.
There is no one else I would rather be with
at the peak as the breeze licks our cheeks.

There is no one else who knows what it means
for me to reach a summit, any summit. You do.
You know the sound my heart makes as we take in the view of the valley.

The Unburying

I stand alone in the cold, shovel in hand,
an easily discernible figure against
the snowy New Jersey day, in a field dotted with gray. Spy
me through the empty, coated trees.

I wonder how to do this unwieldy task.
Where do I start when
the ground has decided it will not yield?
I broke the bones in my body
to unearth what lay beneath my feet:
the skeletons of two boys, entwined
in ways they shouldn't be, a long jagged femur draped
over the pelvis of a smaller figure.

How did they come to be this way, buried
among their great-grandfathers & great-grandmothers?
Pale reflections of the stones stretch out, the white ground filled
with pockets of gold, amber, decay.
Anything that was holds just as much truth
as anything that breathes & walks this earth,
which is to say, what it will tell you
when the dirt has been removed from its mouth.

Memories of My Childhood
(If They Had Been Photographed)

In this one, my brother & I are under the table, scrawling spirals
& twisted shapes we hope will stay hidden, over & over.

Here, we're waiting to get ice cream, melting
in the late summer sun, August almost over.

Sometime later, playing in the parking lot, the smell of bubbling asphalt
filling our nostrils over & over.

We are sprawled out on blank, scratchy carpet, bathed
in the darkness of February.
Mom & Dad drop off boxes at the new house.
He draws my hand
to his penis, which he tells me to tug
over & over & over.

Suddenly, they are calling out from the kitchen below.
We zip up our jeans & jackets, filing downstairs.

What would have happened if they caught us?
What would have followed us out into the icy night?

Love During a Storm, Delighted

Heat lightning, in a flash, inside our bedroom illuminates
the walls, sheets, your olive skin.
My heart dances inside my ribcage at just
the right rhythm for the moment.

I do not float, I do not shrink, I do not cry.
You help me move the way my body wants to move.
When you drag your fingers through my beard, I am
spellbound by your touch, planted nowhere else but here.

To kiss you is to know you—strong, passionate, longing, fierce.
I want to know you more & more
every day for the rest of our lives. Can we sustain this?
A drop of water building on the edge of a leaf, waiting to fall.

Rhapsody in Periwinkle

I find that I delight
in simple pleasures: walking with our beautiful dog, a black muscle car
in canine form, her tags jangling & nails click-clacking
on the sidewalk as we turn toward the woods
abutting the road, the late morning sun warm on our faces, welcoming
us into the reception room of summer, the first one drained
of anxiety in a couple of years, despite a global pandemic.

In this moment I take special notice
of a family of flowers
I have seen nearly every day for the past few weeks, jutting
up amid the tall grass & sprinkled amid the dandelions. I make a beeline
for one, a chicory, & drink in
its beauty. It is an iridescent shade of periwinkle.

I walk toward the flower, leash in hand, & I bend down
to smell it. It does not smell. I count sixteen distinct slender petals,
each fringed with five triangular grooves at the end, separated
like a wooden parapet in a medieval fortress.

I do not need a fortress. I do not need guards. I do not need archers.
I only need to breathe in the light
of this Thursday morning in June.

Late Night Call with God

God's voice echoed through
every house I've ever lived in
& every house I've ever lied in,
whispering, *I don't know how you have done it,*
withstanding the waves & the woods,
the knife & the night,
the stillness of the void.

If You don't know then who does,
I breathed into the stars.
Certainly not me.
I can't even understand how I write these words sometimes,
let alone live.

God replied gently,
Writing & living is plenty.

Our Wedding

> *for Jenny, my wife*

The sand & the sea, glittering.
Lilies, shaking themselves gently in the wind.
The sun reflecting off the Gulf, as it has for millennia.
A chuppah bathed in its glow, rising proudly with its

crystals fluttering in the breeze between the flowers,
glistening with rainbows as the *tallit* cast their shadows
over us, creating a dimple of cool
surrounded by the glare of the late afternoon.
We place rings on each other's fingers,
intoning ancient Hebrew: *Ani l'dodi, v'dodi li—*

I am my beloved's &
my beloved is mine.
The sand & the sea, meeting
as waves recede & return,
rising & falling, constant.

I Find Happiness

Not pure like a first snow, but intense like fire—
in not needing a reckoning to drip from his lips.

In hills that roll on without end,
land untethered to anything familiar, reminders of what was.

The great untangling of my tongue,
letting words gush forth, finally, with aching clarity.

In blank pieces of paper, waiting eagerly
to be filled with new poems, sprouting from my heart like tulips.

In building a new home, free
from the constricting vines of a role that sublimates my soul.

Holding & being held by
someone who accepts me in full, in all that I have been & am.

Her laugh, like sunshine gliding through
trees, beside a refreshing brook that gurgles pleasantly.

Speaking with the fluidity of water,
flowing past down a ravine, a river into an ocean.

We Are the Flowers in That Good Earth

Buried deep in the haunting of our bones
lies, soft & still, the ones we once were & knew & feared for
in foreign beds & hollow, hungry houses.
We survivors sometimes wonder how we got out alive at all.

We know, of course, that there can be a murder scene without blood.
Those are the tricky cases,
the ones that confound hard-boiled detectives for decades.
They rot in the sun like forgotten meat.

We know all of this. We are the
connoisseurs of such a delicacy.
We have felt it become an immutable part of our being,
like a hernia scar or broken tibia that aches in October rainstorms.
But we are so much more than what we buried.

We are the testaments to the fact that gates can rust & not break.
Valleys can yield good earth following avalanches.
Kisses can be reclaimed for ourselves.
Hollowed-out hearts can be refilled, remade, renewed.

The Aftertaste of the Wind

The wind blows & I am unafraid. The earth shudders
beneath my bare toes. I am in a field somewhere out West
beneath a painted sky God would marvel at in wonder.
The breeze kisses the tall grass rhythmically as the day departs.
I wish sometimes I hadn't said a word, but now
there is no going back
to a world that protects monsters & devours boys
like a second dessert, gooey & nauseating.
I open my mouth & wonder at what comes out—
a voice I never truly had: foreign, birdsong in a blizzard,
strong & piercing like an unceasing wind
blowing away illusions spread like tattered cardboard boxes
inside an empty house that is no longer my home.

How to Bury a Boy at Sea

Above us, the sky lost all its natural hue & roared
with a force that shook us from bow to stern.
The time for splintering drew near.

The lightning flashed. For the first time he looked scared.
It was an expression I knew so well, having seen it in the water
staring back at me for years, through every kind of weather.

The waves barked & the wind laughed, for we were children
adrift & aimless like a bubble, one whose very being
could be snuffed out amid the casual violence swirling around us.

Then it happened. The ship began to crack apart.
We were separated, truly, for the first time in memory,
a passenger watching an ancient homeland fade from view.

I was the one who shattered the boat. I was sick of the saltwater
slowly poisoning my cells, depleting me day after day.
First I whispered. Then I spoke. After, I shouted & howled a ferocious tune.

He had caged me here & I had agreed to be caged.
I thought cages were safe. They are not; they are merely a tool
used to keep us from being in our natural state.

He staggered, grasping for me or anything to hold onto,
but scooped up only rain-swept air & disappointment,
precursors to his ultimate watery end.

I was floating on the wreckage as he gulped his last.
I didn't move. I didn't have to. All I had to do was be.
Then he disappeared, a sun forever hiding behind clouds.

There I stood, at last alone, with only one
more body to shed, this boy who lived a lifetime inside of me,
carrying a greater burden than anyone should bear.

This boy slipped out of my skin, billowy & white,
& closed his eyes in peace,
having shown valor beyond measure.

I kissed his forehead, then smoothed his hair & thanked him
for living long enough to see this day, for being
both a boy & something more, something sublime.

He & the boat sank down & I became enveloped
in the water, in grief, in joy, in song. I started to swim
back to shore in the light of the morning.

Acknowledgements

I am grateful to the editors of the following publications where these poems—or versions of these poems—first appeared:

The 2River View
"What Wakes a Mother in the Middle of the Night", "The Sound of Blood Flowing Through Me"

Amethyst Review
"Wandering in Search of Truth", "Late Night Call with God"

Awakened Voices
"The Exorcism of a Boy", "We Are the Flowers in That Good Earth", "The Aftertaste of the Wind"

Constellations
"What the House Sees"

Great Lakes Review
"In the North Country, the Wind Howls Hard"

In Parentheses
"Repayment in Kind", "Starlight"

The Indianapolis Review
"A Note to My Younger Self"

The Laurel Review
"The Lover as Unexpected Glaciologist", "The Unburying"

Linden Avenue Literary Journal
"How to Bury a Boy at Sea"

The Loch Raven Review
"Form & Void", "The Last Act", "Gibraltar"

Moist Poetry Journal
"Fragile"

October Hill Magazine
"The Grief Eater"

Qwerty Magazine
"Memories of My Childhood (If They Had Been Photographed)"

Rust + Moth
"Growth"

Two Peach
"We Never Went to the Beach When I was a Boy"

Thank you to the entire staff of Stillhouse Press for selecting, believing in and helping me shepherd this book into the world. Thank you to Victoria Mendoza, Lindley Estes, Rebecca Burke, Scott Berg, Linda Hall, Alex Horn and Meghan McNamara for your tireless support of this book. Thank you to Douglas Luman for designing such a striking cover image. A special thank you to Tommy Sheffield and Rose Strode, my two dear managing editors, for helping me chisel the stone of my work into a statue, for making me a better poet and for pushing me to make this the best book it could be.

To all of my teachers over the years who encouraged a love of literature and writing and who supported my creative endeavors, including Annie Streiff, Kim Palmiotto, Christina Defeo, Robert Wilson, Winifred Gleason and Christopher Ricks.

To Kimberly Ann Priest, Ruth Awad, José Antonio Rodríguez, Erin Elizabeth Smith, Catherine Pond, Emily Mohn-Slate and Ming Lauren Holden, thank you for being such gracious, attentive and sensitive readers of this collection. Your work and your words mean so very much to me. Thank you also to Dan Kraines for your empathy, friendship and warmth.

To Rachel Mennies, who first looked at the manuscript that become this book and offered invaluable insight, direction, compassion and care. I am forever in your debt, dear friend.

To the group of men who I learned so much from, thank you for your strength, your vulnerability and your indomitable courage. I felt so much freedom in your presence.

To all of the therapists I have worked with, past and present, thank you for helping me to learn that I am not adrift at sea, and that I can make it back to shore and thrive there. I would be lost without your wisdom and care.

To the dear friends and family who I have been blessed to have in my life, thank you for your love and understanding, especially as I was opening up to you about being abused. Those were some of the most difficult months of my life and I am so grateful to have had your support.

To Nick, thank you for being the brother I wish I had.

To Brenna, Grady and Princess, thank you for making me smile every day.

To Jenny, you are my everything. Thank you for your unconditional love.

Resources for Survivors

Rape, Abuse & Incest National Network (RAINN)
      https://www.rainn.org/articles/sexual-assault-men-and-boys

1in6
      https://1in6.org/

National Sexual Violence Resource Center
      https://www.nsvrc.org/working-male-survivors-sexual-violence

Darkness to Light
      https://www.d2l.org/

ISurvive
      https://isurvive.org/

Support for Partners
      https://www.supportforpartners.org

Awakenings
      https://awakeningsart.org/

Elevate|Uplift
      https://www.elevateuplift.org/

ABUSE PREVENTION

Prevent Child Abuse
      https://preventchildabuse.org/what-we-do/child-sexual-abuse-prevention/

Child USA
      https://childusa.org/

Stop It Now
      https://www.stopitnow.org/

The Enough Abuse Campaign
      https://www.enoughabuse.org/

PHIL GOLDSTEIN is a poet, journalist, and senior editor for a content marketing agency. His poetry, which explores the trauma of childhood sexual abuse and the difficult journey to healing that men face, was nominated for a Best of the Net award and has appeared in *The Laurel Review*, *Rust + Moth*, *Two Peach*, *2River View*, *Awakened Voices*, *The Indianapolis Review*, *The Loch Raven Review*, *Linden Avenue Literary Journal*, and *Great Lakes Review*. Phil and his wife, Jenny, live in Alexandria, Virginia, with Brenna the dog, and cats Grady and Princess. *How to Bury a Boy at Sea* is his debut poetry collection.

This book would not have been possible
without the hard work of our staff.

We would like to acknowledge:

ROSE STRODE	Managing Editor
ALEX HORN	Director, Publicity & Marketing
LINDA HALL	Operations Manager
SCOTT BERG	Publisher
GREGG WILHELM	Editorial Advisor, MFA Director, GMU
MEGHAN McNAMARA	Marketing & Media Advisor, Founding Editor

STILL
HOUSE
PRESS

CPSIA information can be obtained
at www.ICGtesting.com
Printed in the USA
LVHW062003290322
714730LV00015B/783